BIRTH OF A BULLY

Birth of a Bully

Companion short story to
Vows of Revenge

JF Ridgley

RPride Publishing
Birth of a Bully

ISBN: 978-1-951269-10-4 ebook

ISBN: 978-1-951269-11-1 Print

Cover design - Cathy Helms http://Avalongraphics.org

**Other Books and stories
by JF Ridgley**

Historical Fiction
Vows of Revenge
Birth of a Bully

VULCAN'S WRATH SERIES
Threatened Loyalties
For the Family

AGRICOLA SERIES
Red Fury – Revolt
Chrysalis
Contemporary Romance
Love Backwards
18 Wheeler

Chapter 1

"THEY WHAT?"

Cassius's young heart stopped as his father glared at his muddy, torn tunic and then slowly, very slowly, the man's glare climbed up to the boy's face. It always scared him when his father's face got this red and angry, like the night he beat his mother because she disobeyed him. Tears collected in his eyes.

Cassius blinked to keep them hidden. His papa didn't like crybabies. "Ste-Stephiano s-shoved me in a p-puddle. And…and stuck my face in the m-mud." Once they started, the words came easier "He said…if I ever come back…on their lands, he'll…he'll really…hurt me."

His father set hard fists on his hips. He was shorter than most men, but was twice as thick. Yet, at moments like this, he seemed as big as Poseidon's sea monster, the Kraken. "That. Land. Is. Our. Land, Boy," spat from the man's lips. The inspection intensified in his glare. "And what in Hades were you doing there?"

Young Cassius shoved his chest out bravely. "I wasn't doing n-nothing, Papa. Nothing. I…I was only trying to catch rabbits. For dinner. You know, hunting…for rabbits…for dinner." He didn't dare tell his father that he had disobeyed him and had ridden Nikitus when he wasn't supposed to. Nor that he'd fondled Stephiano's sister to find out why his father enjoyed doing that to the slave girls. When Stephania screamed, within seconds, her brothers had appeared out of nowhere.

When his father stormed across the atrium, flinging his arms to the ceiling, Cassius started breathing again. "Fucking plebes! The gods have willed what we stand above them. But, they all think they're equal to us." His father halted by the impluvium bubbling with water and wheeled about. "Cassius Julius Gullus."

Terror sliced through the boy's insides at the sound of his full name. Every muscle turned to stone as his father marched back across the room with a finger pointed directly him.

"I expect you to see that no plebe ever shoves your face in mud ever again. You hear me." His father halted close enough for the man's finger to draw Cassius's eyes together. His voice dropped dangerously low as did his bushy eyebrows. "And *you* will see that this plebe eats shit. Am I clear?"

"I will, Papa. I will. I'll make him…eat shit." Cassius nodded vigorously as urine leaked into his loincloth.

The finger withdrew into a fist. "No one humiliates or disrespects the house of Cassius Julius Gullus. Don't you ever forget that. Because I won't," bellowed from his father's lips. The hand dropped to his father's side. For what seemed an eternity, his father stood there, glaring down as if to drill the command deeper, and then he wheeled about to disappear into the rear garden.

A vast wall loomed where the man had been standing. Cassius backed away from it. "How can I make Stephiana and her brothers 'eat shit'?"

After all, Stephiana's oldest brother Stephiano was fourteen, six years older than he was. And so were the middle brothers who were twelve and ten. Stephiana and her twin brother, the youngest Stephiano, were eight years old like he was.

Cassius wished he could cut them all into pieces and throw them in the well. Or…or order Papa's soldiers to destroy everything the Stephiano family rented from his father. His father would never approve of destroying anything he owned.

Desperation rose like sharp thorns, tearing at his insides. Nobody listened to him anyway. He studied the slaves standing along the walls, eyes cast downward, hands clasped before them. None of them would tell him what to do. They were all dumb anyway. To them, he was nothing but a stupid boy. And now he had to teach a bunch of plebes a lesson to not mess with patricians.

And if he didn't, his father would beat him as he had beaten his mother.

If she had been there, she would see that everything would be all right. He ground his fists around his eye sockets to press the reemerging tears back to where they belonged. *Why did she have to run away?*

He studied his personal slave waiting beside a bedroom door. Lumar had kept his hand over Stephiana's mouth, grinning as she squirmed. But the stupid girl bit him, and the slave let her scream. So, this was his fault.

Cassius crossed the atrium and slapped the young slave across the face. Hearing the him cry out excited him. He hit Lumar again. And again, until the boy fell to the floor and curled up like a baby.

Delight thrilled through Cassius's veins. Maybe this was why his father beat the slaves so often. He considered using the lash but didn't know where it was. So, instead, he just kicked the slave in the ribs and went on into the bedroom.

Chapter 2

"WHAT ARE YOU doing here?"

Cassius's attention shot up through the ripe wheat at Stephiana holding a water jug on her hip. She had found him hiding in the wheat field as she went to the water well nearby.

He and Lumar stood up, brushing the grass and dirt from their tunics. "None of your business, you filthy plebe." Cassius set his fists on his hips like his father did. "And… and you can't stop me…from being here. This is Papa's land."

"We rent it, so it's ours." She set the jug on the ground. "And my brothers said you better not ever come here again."

"They don't scare me." His heart slammed against his rib cage with the lie.

"Really?" A smirk slid across her face. Her blood-curdling scream filled the air. Her gaze locked with his as she grabbed the neck of her tunic , ripping it across her chest. "Don't! Go away! NO! Help! Stephiano, help me!"

Grape leaves suddenly started rustling as if something the size of the Minotaur was charging through the vineyard.

Lumar fidgeted beside Cassius. "Dominus, let's go."

The slave had a wonderful idea. Together, they bolted through the tall wheat. Cassius barely made the ridge when hard hands caught his shoulders and shoved him face-first to the dirt. He rolled over and looked up at the four smug faces of the Stephiano brothers gathering around him.

Like their sister, all four brothers had dark brown hair, mean brown eyes, and were lanky no matter what their ages. "Stephiana, get back to the house while we take care of this little shit. And keep Papa busy," the oldest Stephiano ordered. "You, hold his slave while we tie the little bastard up."

He really wanted to hurt them as he had Lumar. But, Stephiano's shadow spread over him, sucking every bit of his courage away. Cassius scrambled to his feet. "I…I didn't do nothin' to your sister."

"Doesn't matter." Stephiano grinned and stood there: hands on hips, legs spread. "Remember what I said I'd do if you ever came back on our land?"

"This is my land. Papa said I can go anywhere I want, you fucking plebe."

Cassius swung a fist at the taller boy's face and missed. The plebe's calloused hand caught it and yanked him back into the dirt. "I wouldn't be so sure of that, not if you are a smart, fucking patrician. And obviously, you aren't."

Warm urine pooled between Cassius's legs and seeped into the dirt.

"Look, the little shit wet himself." Stephiana's twin brother yelled. Laughter roared around Cassius as the older brother dropped a knee between his shoulder blades.

Lumar stood there like a helpless baby while the twelve-year-old brother held a pruning knife at his throat. "Best listen to our brother, you little shit."

Cassius glared at Lumar. "Do something, you stupid slave or I'll tell Papa!"

Panic blazed from Lumar's eyes from either the threat of his father or the pruning knife biting into his flesh below his jaw. But the slave made no attempt to fight or help him.

They weren't supposed to do this to him. He was a patrician. "Let go, you filthy plebe or my father will kill you. Let go. Now!"

"Your piss-ant father? That short turd who thinks because he's a patrician, we plebes have to tremble?" Stephiano slapped the top of Cassius's head and pulled something from his belt.

"I said if you ever touched my sister again, I'd hurt you. So, I'm gonna cut your hands off for touching her." He looked up at his brothers. "Help me hold him."

Cassius squirmed to find a way out from under Stephiano's knee as the two remaining brothers gripped his arms and stretched them above his head.

Stephiano tossed the knife back and forth in his hands. "Hold him good. He's gonna squeal like a pig."

Not his hands. No, not his hands. "No. Please. I won't come back. I won't. Please. I never touched your sister. I'll never—"

"What's going on here?"

Stephiano bolted to his feet as his brothers let go and stiffened to attention. "Nothing Papa."

Cassius rolled over to see the elder Stephiano, a freedman, standing there like Jupiter. The weathered man scanned everything before him. "I asked you a question, boy."

Stephiano wilted under his father's gaze. "Just scaring this little shit from ever touching Stephiana ever again He ripped her tunica like before. I...I sent her back to the house."

"I did not," Cassius climbed to his feet, rubbing his wrists. He wiggled his fingers at his side, enjoying the precious movement. "She…she tore it herself."

"Oh yeah. Then why'd she scream." Stephiano snarled and drew back a fist, ready to sling it.

"I'll take care of this." Stephiano's father stepped between his son and Cassius. "Go on. Get back to work, or I'll take a belt to all of ya." Throwing demonic glances back over their shoulders, the boys shuffled toward the vineyards. The man's deep brown gaze settled sternly on Cassius. But not mean. Not red like his own father. "What were you doin' here, boy?"

Lumar still stood there like a useless fool. Cassius straightened his tunic and smelled the dirty urine tracks coating his legs. "I didn't touch your daughter. She tore her tunic."

"Tunics can be fixed."

Cassius stiffened to attention and tried to be equal to the towering man. "Papa said I can walk anywhere I want, even here. And…and, I was just looking for…him." Cassius pointed at Lumar who suddenly came to attention. "He…he ran away. I found him…here messing with your girl."

"Well, you got your slave. Now, I suggest going back to your fine patrician's villa and stay there. We have work to get done for your father. Now go. Get on back. " The man shoved Cassius's shoulder as if to nudge him on his way.

Cassius slapped the calloused hand aside. "Don't touch me. I'm a… You aren't allowed to touch me."

The man smirked. "Then, don't give me cause. Tell your father I'll have his soon enough."

"I…I will." Cassius stood straight, puffing his chest out. "I will." Yes. That was good. He could tell Papa about the grain.

CHAPTER 3

CASSIUS WAVED THE fruit away. He missed his mother serving them. Now, Lumar had to serve the food. At least, the rod had been enough to make the slave tremble as he held the tray. Punishing a slave was really exhausting.

His father studied the welts over Lumar's arms and legs. Even the slave's face. "What's wrong with him?"

"I beat him. He…he didn't do as I told him."

His father bit into the crisp peach slice with relish and motioned Lumar away. "They don't listen unless you beat them." He sucked the honey from his fingers and rested back on the dining lounger. "The longer plebes or slaves have their way, the more brazen they get, as you have seen. "Have you settled this matter?""

"Soon, Papa. I…I will soon."

"Good. You need to do something soon, or they will never respect you." The moon beamed through the atrium opening in the ceiling as his father drifted off in thought. "I remember a time when that bastard Lucianus tried to mess with me." A sly smile emerged on the man's face. "Now, I own that plebe's lands."

"What'd Lucianus do?"

"Thought he could tell me to leave his land like Stephiano's boy did you." His father sipped his wine and dropped a deliberate gaze. "And that's why you have to take care of this yourself, Cassius, as I had to do. Do you know how you plan to take care of those plebes yet?" his father asked.

Cassius looked into his goblet, as his guts twisted and vomit rose into his throat. "I'm working on a plan." A lie. He had nothing. Yet that *nothing* lurked even in the shadows like a demon.

His father sighed heavily. "Sometimes you just have to beat it into them like you did Lumar." He set his wine down on the table, rose, and then turned. "So, I expect you see to this done… very soon."

"I will, Papa."

Chapter 4

"WHAT'S THAT?" CASSIUS asked and stepped from Nikita's stall to see what the barn slave had on the shovel. The old slave offered the scoop of the half-eaten remains of two rats that had to be days old. The smell of rotting carcasses assaulted Cassius's senses. Even the horse snorted at the smell of death.

"Dead rats, dominus."

Cassius waved the slave away and went back into the horse's stall where the four-year-old stallion pawed the fresh straw and jerked at the rope tie. Nikitus had been a gift from his father for Saturnalia. Frustration ate at the boy's nerves as he stroked the horse's soft black coat.

His father had promised to teach him how to ride. But, he was always too busy because of that big hole he wanted dug between his and Lucianus's villas. If it weren't for that, his father would be able to teach him how to ride. He wished Gennadius hadn't run away with his mother. The master slave had always had time to help him. He was never too busy.

Cassius walked out of the stall. Maybe he shouldn't have lied to his father by denying that the master slave had saved him from falling off Nikitus when the animal had reared. Then, maybe his mother and Gennadius would still be there.

He kicked a cat strolling past the stall. He wished it were that easy to punish Stephiano. Cassius rubbed his wrist where the pruning blade had nicked him. If he didn't do something soon, his father would really get angry. He didn't want to think about that. He just had to find a way to…

The rats!

All he had to do was drop the stinking rats in Stephiano's well and, as they rotted, they'd poison the water, and the family would get sick and die. That would teach those plebes. Relief sang through him.

"Get those dead rats."

Lumar jolted from the dividing wall where he had been leaning. "What…dominus?"

"You heard me. Get them."

CHAPTER 5

NIKITA KEPT SNATCHING at the bit and trotting in the darkness of predawn. Cassius had to circle the stupid horse around Lumar to keep the animal at a walk. The slave looked like a dark shadow running beside him. No matter how much he had beaten Lumar, the stupid slave refused to throw the rats in the well for him. "No! I won't do it."

The only choice he had now was to do it himself. He could. He could. Yes.

Everything had started well. The night before, Lumar had helped him sacrifice a cat to Mars. He guessed that the red guts were a good omen. Then, hours before dawn, they managed to blindfold Nikita to keep the horse quiet until they got beyond the villa walls.

Now, all he had to do was ride up to the well, drop the rats down that dark stone throat, and gallop away before anyone saw him.

And wait for Stephiano's family to die.

Thoughts of their funeral flashed through Cassius's mind. A smile eased across his face, as he pictured himself pretending to be stunned when the whole family had simply died strangely. He could already see the satisfied smile on his father's face. His father would be so proud that he had made the plebes "eat shit." *Or drink it.* Excitement thrilled through him.

Then his blood chilled. What if it all went wrong? What if Nikita reared and he fell into the well? Who would help him out? What if no one found him and he drowned?

Cassius clutched the reins and Nikita reared. He grabbed the black mane to stay on and then circled the horse to make the stallion walk again. Maybe he should leave the horse with Lumar and sneak up to the well. Go on foot. The new plan felt better. Yes. He could do that. He would do that.

The mile marker appeared in the timid dawn. Cassius halted the horse, slid down onto the stone, and handed the reins to the slave. "Give me the filthy shit?"

"Yes, dominus." Lumar lifted the rancid bag from his side. Its stink was strong enough to twist anyone's insides as Cassius took the bag.

"Wait here no matter what, or I'll lash you like Papa did Gennadius."

"I will, dominus. May the gods see you victorious."

Every step toward the ridge was laden with concrete. At the summit, Cassius belly-crawled over the top, dragging the rats behind him. Fortunately, the wind blew the smell toward Lumar.

Like a sign from the gods, dawn peaked over the tips of the distant mountains and dimly lit the well. Encouraged, Cassius worked down the rise, cautious of every step, every sound. He stopped to listen for a dog to bark, anything that would alert the Stephiano brothers. Nothing.

He replayed what he had to do. Get to the well, toss the rats in, and run like Mercury to get back to Nikita to get home before his father found them gone. Cassius's heart thundered so hard he couldn't breathe. Sweat broke out over his entire body as he collapsed against the damp, cold stones. The musky smell of the cool water drifted to him. He'd made it.

He rose up on his knees and scanned the shadows of the distant barn. The nearby shed. The house further on. All silent. Nothing moved. He dropped the rats into the looming black pit, and relished the splash that greeted his ears.

Just as he turned to flee back to the ridge, a voice cut through the shadows. "Well, look who's back."

CHAPTER 6

CASSIUS'S HEART FROZE in his chest as four shadows appeared from the far side of the well and surrounded him like ghosts. He pushed past the youngest, but Stephiano tossed him back to the well like a sack of grain. "What'd' ya drop in our well, you little shit?" Stephiano asked.

"Yeah? What'd' ya drop in there?" the others echoed.

"Nothing. Let me go." Cassius tried darting through a gap between the middle brothers, but Stephiano clutched the neck of Cassius's tunic.

"Then, what splashed?"

"Yeah. What splashed?"

Cassius glared up at his captor. "It was a stupid fish or something, you filthy plebe."

"Or maybe our little patrician threw some rotting rats in there, and he wants to go fishing for them."

Panic ripped through Cassius. *How did they know about the rats?* "Lumar! Help me! Lumar!"

The second brother laughed. "Your slave boy told us what you had planned to do, so you better not touch him or we will kill you. Got that"

Oh, I will kill Lumar for this. Or…or his father would. Cassius jerked loose and, for a breath, he was free. "Get out of my way."

Just a few steps from the well, a foot tripped him and he slammed face down onto the packed dirt. Stephiano set his foot between his shoulder blades. "You're not going anywhere, except after those rats, you little shit. Tie those ropes around his ankles."

"No!" Even as Cassius kicked and thrashed, the brothers slipped a noose around each ankle. Then Stephiano lifted Cassius by his tunic and slammed him against the well stones.

"You are going after those rats. Understand, you little shit? Or you won't be going go home ever again."

Cassius hugged the wooden support of the well like life itself. He struggled desperately to kick the ropes free, but they were too tight around his ankles. "I didn't throw anything in there. I didn't!"

The brothers peeled Cassius's arms away from the wood and then lifted him from the ground. With one heave, he dropped into the well's stone throat. The dark shadows and smells of the musky mold enfolded him as he fell backward through the black abyss.

His scream had to wake the gods. They preferred patricians. His father said so. They had to help him. He saw his mother's beaten face. He saw Gennadius dying on the lashing pole. He saw his father's furious glare burning from his eyes. An eternity drifted past him until he fell into the wet, velvet darkness and air sucked from his lungs.

His bulla smacked him in the eye as he swam to the surface. Little good the childhood necklace was at protecting him. Spitting the cold crisp liquid from his mouth, Cassius slapped for something solid to hold onto. All he found was the frigid water.

"Found 'em," echoed from above.

Found what? The rats. By the gods, they were in there with him. He had to find them or they would let him die down here and no one would ever find him. Not his father. No one. And he never would be able to beat Lumar for telling them everything.

"Get me out of here you stupid plebes! My father will kill you for this."

The ropes around his ankles shifted and he was dragged through the water until his tunic slithered up his legs, over his belly, and covered his face like a wet pillow. His bulla tangled over his ears and then fell into the black depths as he was lifted upwards and hung just above the water.

"Got them? Didn't think so."

They dropped him. Then they dragged him up again. Laughter echoed off the walls as Cassius was, again, dropped. This time his tunic slid over his arms and face to completely disappear in the freezing water. Frozen muscles cramped in his stomach as the frigid water plunged up his nose, piercing his head like a knife.

Cassius wiped his face with his wet arms and lashed through the water for anything to hold onto. Nothing. And the stupid rats were likely at the bottom now. He'd never find them. He was going to die there. His only warmth were his tears.

When he tried to breathe, something nudged against his ear and floated into his gaping mouth. The taste and smell of rotting flesh gagged him. He slapped filth away. Then he realized what that was and reached for the carcasses. But they evaded his grasp as if taunting him.

Stenched-filled water flooded his nose as, again, he was drawn upward. "Find 'em? Guess not." They let go of the ropes.

Cold water smacked his face again, sending waves against the slime coated stones. Freezing fingers gripped his flesh. Cassius exhaled snot out of both nostrils and spread the mucus over his lips as he slapped the black depths for the rats. Where were those fucking rats? They had to be…

A rotted carcass brushed against his wrist. The knotted slimy tails filled his fist. "I g-got them! I g-got them!" exploded from his shivering mouth.

Once again, the rope started jerking him upward. His heart slammed in his chest as he clung to the slimy, wormy tails. Finally, the warmth of dawn settled over his shivering body like a blanket.

"Yeah, I guess he got 'em." Stephiano retrieved the rats. "Oops." The rat caucuses fell past Cassius's cheek and disappeared back into the black darkness. "Guess you gotta go fishing again, you filthy patrician."

"No. Please. Let me out of here. Please."

"Sorry. We can't. If we leave them in there, my family might die." Stephiano grabbed him by his hair and lifted his face so Cassius could see the smirk gleaming on his lips. "You wouldn't like that, now would you?

"No. No. I wouldn't."

"So, you gotta go back and get them."

One shove and Cassius felt swallowed by the black depths. The water slapped like a fist and then enfolded him. Hatred finer than gold burned, as he fought his way to the surface and flailed about for the rats.

He no longer cared that they were rotten, if they were half eaten, or that their organs dangled from their skeletons. All he really wanted now was to see Lumar and all the Stephiano brothers dead for this. His hand smacked one rat and seized the tied tails. "G-G-Got 'em."

"Both of them?"

"Y-Yes…"

Choking and snorting, he rose upward. Suddenly, he dropped back into the water, lifted, dropped, lifted. The water slapped his face and flooded into his nose. The taste of the rat guts poured into his mouth.

Finally, little by little, jerk by jerk, his body rose. Stones passed before Cassius's face and then his body felt the cherished warmth welcoming him out of the frigid depths. The savoring scent of dry earth and ripe grain blew over Cassius.

"Dammit, he's got 'em," one of the brothers said. The rest laughed.

Cassius threw the rats over the wall and into the dirt. The motion dangled him from the wooden crossbeam like a carcass ready for slaughter. "Don't drop them in again. Please don't. Please."

A cough sounded in the distance, drawing all four gazes toward it. "Papa!"

The brothers slung Cassius over the well wall, and dropped him to the dirt—the precious dry, warm dirt—and fled into the nearby vineyard.

The sun kissed the mountain ridges, as Cassius worked his frozen fingers and yanked the loops from his ankles. Alas one rope fell free and then the other. His feet, as blue as bruises, flooded feeling to his toes like a thousand bee stings.

He didn't care what his father thought now. He simply wanted to go home. Home. And once Papa knew what they had done, he would see the Stephiano family were punished proper. And Lumar would pay with his life for tattling everything to Stephiano's brother.

Pain streaked through Cassius's legs when he stood and stumbled back against the well stones. Fear struck as if the black fingers would reach and drag him into the frigid pit. Cassius heaved away, staggering like his father when he was too drunk. The thoughts of punishing Lumar kept him moving, stirred each muscle to life.

The morning sun broke over the distant mountain revealing the stone marker where Nikita remained tied to the post. But, no Lumar. The slave was gone. Raw anger welled deeper than black abyss. Whatever his father ever felt against Gennadius, now coiled through Cassius's muscles. He'd find that stupid slave and he'd pay for this.

Nikitus startled and plunged backward when he grabbed the reins, almost yanking the leather reins from Cassius's grip. He needed to get home before his father got up. He stroked the horse's neck the way Gennadius always did to calm an animal. Finally, the stupid horse let him climb up onto the stone marker and scramble onto its warm back.

Then, the horse wheeled as if stung and bolted off toward home. The reins dropped from Cassius's grasp, so he grabbed for the mane. A stonewall marking his father's land came closer with each stride.

"No! Stop! Stop!"

Obviously, the horse was going to jump it. He had never been on a horse when it jumped. The wall rose before him like a mountain. Suddenly the horse simply lifted and floated into the air as if it had become Pegasus and they were flying.

The mystical view lasted in slow motion allowing Cassius to see the world like a bird, and then it disappeared when the horse plunged downward and landed hard. Everything twisted and jerked beneath him. Cassius flew from the horse's back and slammed into a loose pile of stones. Pain fired into his skull and the world turned as dark as the well.

Patrician. Piece of shit. Plebe. You got them? I expect you to take care of these bastards. No son of mine will…, I will, Papa. Your slave boy told us you were coming. You won't go home until you do. The insults changed to high-pitched screams. The darkness changed to a vision of a pink sky. Cassius sat up, his head spinning. He couldn't focus. Every bone in his back felt broken. Something moved beside him. Something alive. *Rats. Big Rats.*

Panic jerked Cassius to his feet. The rasping screams drew his attention to Nikita thrashing in the pile of stones. "Get up you stupid horse." He grabbed the reins and jerked. "Get up."

The horse ignored him, just as everyone did. Yet something looked odd about the horse's left front leg. It looked crooked. So did its back leg, as if it were caught in a pile of rocks.

Cassius's insides cringed as he realized the horse couldn't get up. If the horse didn't get up, his father would beat him for disobeying him, for riding when he had been told not to. Images of his father's face rose like a demon. The red glare. The sick smile. The hard fists. Terror encased Cassius. And he beat him because he'd failed to make Stephiano eat shit and lied about everything.

Fear, colder than the well, dug sharp claws around his heart. He couldn't go back home. He had to go somewhere where his father couldn't find him. But where?

The stones blushed with the new dawn, driving the dark shadows beneath the distant trees. Wherever Lumar had gone. Anywhere but home.

Cassius searched the rock-filled vista for a place to escape. Galleys. Yes. The only place his father wouldn't search for him was down at the wharf where the galleys docked. He could become a pirate. He'd sneak onto a galley and go everywhere they did.

Hope swelled like a breath of blessed air. And…and maybe one day, he'd find Lumar and his mother and they'd be happy again.

Fini

Does Cassius find his mother….find out in

VOWS OF REVENGE…

Late summer, Stabianum, Italy, 295 B.C.

Chapter 1

"H E'S COMING! HE'S coming!"

Aelia's heart chilled as she twisted the iron wedding band on her left hand. *He's coming.* She didn't want her husband coming home.

Her seven-year-old son raced toward her, eyes glowing with excitement. A cold shiver slid down her spine as she squatted before him. "How far away is…your father?"

"Not far," young Cassius gasped. She brushed away the beads of sweat clinging to the dark curls stuck to his forehead on this dry, hot summer day. "Not far, Mama. I saw the dust from the horses. There must be thousands with him!"

She studied the round beaming face of her son as she adjusted the childhood protective charm on his necklace. *He looks so like his father. I just pray he does not grow to be not like him.*

"Do you suppose he's brought the whole army with him?" she asked. An ounce of hope ignited in her heart. If Cassius brought his soldiers, he'd be too busy for her.

"I hope so, Mama. Maybe I can go riding with them."

Aelia scowled. "Young Cassius Julius Gullus, you'll do no such thing." Gennadius, her master slave, only recently taught him how to ride. At seven, the boy considered himself quite the equestrian. "You are not to ride until your father says you may do so. Do you understand?"

"Yes, Mama."

Aelia glanced at the boy's personal slave, who stood nearby. "See that he is prepared to meet his father." She looked down at her son. *He must be perfect. Perfect.* "Now go. Be quick. You must not disappoint your father."

"Yes Mama."

The slave scurried off behind the boy.

Aelia's stomach tightened even more as she scanned the atrium, the formal greeting room, for some flaw, for some overlooked error, anything. All she saw were fresh white curtains ruffling over the doorways to the back garden. The hot sunlight beamed through the opening in the ceiling onto the pool, which was filled with spewing water from the cistern below the pristine limestone floor.

A breeze full of herbal fragrances drifted through the potted palms and ferns boasting no dead leaves. She gazed across atrium through the four columns and studied the two couches before the tablinum, the official office that faced the vestibule where she stood. She went to one couch and straightened it an inch. *Perfect. Everything is to be perfect.*

Her heart thundered against her ribs. Cassius's letter arrived last week and, in that moment, all joy faded from her soul. For the last three years, her husband had fought with Rome against the Samnites and now, was coming home victorious. And Cassius Julius Gullus liked being victorious....

About the Author

I love the ancient world. Even after years of researching and many trips to the sites of my stories, I am still fascinated by what I find for my next story. I love bringing this world to life in my award-winning stories of power, greed, violence, and love.

Be sure to stop by my website to discover more about my stories also sign up for my newsletter so you never miss what's coming next **http://www.jfridgley.com** Be assured that I do not share your address or send an excessive barrage of information.

I would love to hear from you so drop me a note at **jfridgley@jfridgley.com**

www.ingramcontent.com/pod-product-compliance
Lightning Source LLC
Chambersburg PA
CBHW032045180726
48284CB00008B/2770